#6 Beetle Blast

Books in the S.W.I.T.C.H. series

#6 Beetle Blast

Ali Sparkes

illustrated by
Ross Collins

darbycreek

MINNEAPOLIS

Darby Creek
A division of Lerner Publishing Group, Inc.
241 First Avenue North
Minneapolis, MN 55401 U.S.A.

Website address: www.lernerbooks.com

Main body text set in ITC Goudy Sans Std. 14/19.
Typeface provided by Monotype Typography.

Library of Congress Cataloging-in-Publication Data

Sparkes, Ali.
        Beetle blast / by Ali Sparkes ; illustrated by Ross Collins.
            p.   cm. — (S.W.I.T.C.H. ; #06)
        Summary: On a trip to a pond with a local nature group, twins Josh and Danny accidentally eat a muffin laced with Petty Potts' SWITCH spray and are transformed into very stinky beetles.
        ISBN 978-0-7613-9204-0 (lib. bdg. : alk. paper)
        [1. Beetles—Fiction. 2. Brothers—Fiction. 3. Twins—Fiction.
4. Science fiction.] I. Collins, Ross, ill. II. Title.
PZ7.S73712Bee 2013
        [Fic]—dc23   2012026637

Manufactured in the United States of America
1 – SB – 12/31/12

For Freddie (junior)

Danny and Josh
(and Piddle)

They may be twins, but they're NOT the same! Josh loves insects, spiders, beetles, and bugs. Danny can't stand them. Anything little with multiple legs freaks him out. So sharing a bedroom with Josh can be . . . erm . . . interesting. Mind you, they both love putting earwigs in big sister Jenny's underwear drawer . . .

Danny
- FULL NAME: Danny Phillips
- AGE: eight years
- HEIGHT: taller than Josh
- FAVORITE THING: skateboarding
- WORST THING: creepy-crawlies and cleaning
- AMBITION: to be a stuntman

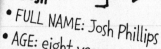

Josh

- FULL NAME: Josh Phillips
- AGE: eight years
- HEIGHT: taller than Danny
- FAVORITE THING: collecting insects
- WORST THING: skateboarding
- AMBITION: to be an entomologist

Piddle

- FULL NAME: Piddle the dog Phillips
- AGE: two dog years (fourteen in human years)
- HEIGHT: not very
- FAVORITE THING: chasing sticks
- WORST THING: cats
- AMBITION: to bite a squirrel

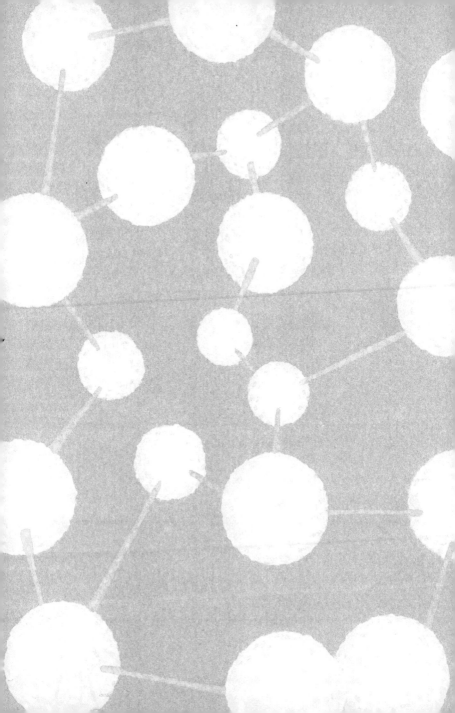

Contents

Let Them Eat Cake

By the time the toxic cloud reached him it was already too late. Josh went cross-eyed. He grabbed his throat and gurgled. He slumped onto the bed. His face went purple.

"Mmm—mmm—mo—" he rasped. His poisoner stood over him, smirking. He was immune to the gas.

"Mo—" gasped Josh, falling off the bed and crawling toward the door. "MOM! Danny's farting at me again!"

Danny grinned proudly. His twin brother fell out onto the landing, sucking in grateful breaths of clean air.

Mom was less amused. She put her head around their bedroom door. She withdrew again quickly.

"Danny! That's revolting! Go to the bathroom at once!" she called from the other side of the door. "Good grief! What is going on in your innards?"

"You feed me," pointed out Danny.

"Don't be smart!" snapped Mom.

"It's OK—I've stopped now," said Danny. He stepped out to see his twin slumped against the banister. Josh flapped a hand in front of his face.

"Well, I hope so!" said Mom. "I don't want

you embarrassing Josh at the Wild Things meeting."

Danny blinked in surprise. "Wild Things? I don't go to Wild Things! *I'm* not the freaky little bug geek. That's just Josh!"

Josh was identical to Danny on the outside (although a lot less fluffy on the hair front and without the skater-boy clothes). But on the inside, the brothers couldn't have been more different. Danny loved loud music, skateboarding, and kicking soccer balls around. Josh loved peering at nature through a magnifying glass. That's why Josh had signed up for Wild Things. He went every week with a bunch of other freaky little bug geeks. Danny had no intention of joining him!

"I'm sorry, but you *have* to go," said Mom. She took some towels into the bathroom. "Your soccer coach called to say practice is canceled. I'm going to pick up my new car. There's nobody to look after you. You're going with Josh."

"Oh *no*!" wailed Josh. "He's going to fart all the way through!"

"Ah well," sighed Danny. "I'll just have to set up my own Wild Things gang—the Stink Bugs."

"Just *try* to act interested," hissed Josh as he and Danny joined the other Wild Things at the Blackthorn Wildlife Center. They met every Monday after school. They did experiments, nature hikes, and looked at things through microscopes. Today they were going pond dipping to see what they could find.

"Danny, meet Ollie, Milo, Biff, and Poppy," said Josh. He pointed to each of his fellow bug geeks in turn. They all wore "nature freak" clothes, Danny noticed. Lots of green and brown and little vests with lots of pockets. Just like Josh. Danny, in his bright orange sweatshirt and baseball cap, looked like a traffic cone by a hedge.

"Hi, Danny," said Biff. He had a pair of binoculars around his neck.

"Greetings," said Ollie and Milo, together. They both had glasses and funny green hats, just like old people wore.

"Hi, Danny, nithe to meet you," lisped Poppy. She had brown braids, freckles, and a rather alarming number of teeth. She rattled a little plastic tub at him. She whispered, "Antth' eggths!" with her eyebrows going up and down.

"Er . . . yeah," said Danny, backing away.

"Look—Granddadth come to help today," said Poppy. She pointed to a tall man in a low-brimmed hat who was standing nearby, gazing out the window. Danny noticed he had a strange, black, pointed fingernail on the little finger of his left hand. Well, weirdness obviously ran in the family.

"I think she likes you," sniggered Josh. Poppy smiled scarily at Danny and stroked the lid of her plastic tub. "She wants to take you home . . ."

"Shut up!" hissed Danny. He hurried away toward some interesting buttons near a collection of wildlife pictures. They made wildlife-y noises when he pressed them. *Ribbit.* "Toad," said Danny. Chirrup. "Grasshopper," said Danny. Zzzzzzz. "Bluebottle."

"See," said Josh. "You're quite good at this stuff."

"Only because . . ." said Danny, ". . . we've either been one of them or nearly been *eaten* by one of them."

"Shhhh!" hissed Josh, looking around uneasily. "Don't tell everyone!"

"What? That our crazy next-door neighbor keeps turning us into creepy-crawlies?" said Danny, making no effort at all to be quiet. "Yeah, right. Everyone's going to believe *that*!"

Someone poked Danny hard in the ribs and said, "Shhhhh, you numbskull! You never know who might be listening! And I am not crazy. I am a genius!"

Danny and Josh spun around, gaping with shock. There stood Petty Potts, the old lady from next door. She was wearing a tweedy hat and glasses, carrying a straw bag and smiling sweetly. You would never guess what she

truly was. A brilliant scientist with a secret laboratory hidden beneath her garden shed! Earlier that year Josh and Danny had stumbled into it. She was in the middle of one of her astonishing experiments—to change things into creepy-crawlies.

They had gotten caught up in a jet of her S.W.I.T.C.H. spray and shortly afterward morphed into spiders. That was a bit of a shock. It was a small miracle that they hadn't been squashed flat, drowned, or eaten. And since then, despite trying really hard to steer clear of any further spraying, they had each been turned into a bluebottle, a grasshopper, an ant, and a crane fly. Thankfully, only temporarily.

"What are *you* doing here?" spluttered Josh.

"It's a free country!" said Petty. "I'm allowed into my local wildlife center, aren't I?"

Danny eyed her bag nervously, looking for the telltale plastic spray bottle.

"You needn't look so petrified, Danny!" she said. "I haven't got any S.W.I.T.C.H. spray with me today."

Danny sighed with relief. It wasn't so much the "being a creepy-crawly" he minded. More the "nearly being eaten" so very often. He'd also once spent more time than he wanted to remember hiding in a cat's ear while he was a grasshopper. And he was haunted still by the things he'd eaten when he was a bluebottle.

"No," said Petty, reaching into her bag and pulling out a small tin. "No spray today. This time it's in pellet form. I want to S.W.I.T.C.H. a rat. I need to try out more mammals—other than you two. I'm going to hide the pellets in some food!" She leaned in toward them and whispered. "Don't forget to keep looking out for the REPTOSWITCH cube! Only one more to find." She looked edgily around her. "And never forget you might be being watched! Victor Crouch's people are everywhere!" And she strode off, before Danny or Josh could say anything else.

Josh shrugged. "Well, at least there's no chance we'll get fooled by *pellets*," he said. "Let's just pretend we don't know her."

19

"She's never going to let up about that blinkin' cube, is she?" muttered Danny. "We've found four of them, and she already had one. You'd think she'd be happy with that!"

"Yes—but without the *last* cube, she can't figure out the REPTOSWITCH code, can she?" said Josh. "And without the code she'll never be able to make the spray. And we'll never get a chance to be alligators or snakes."

Josh and Danny looked at each other and bit their identical lips. Most of their adventures as creepy-crawlies had been terrifying. But they'd also been exciting and, at times, quite awesome. Both boys knew how it felt to fly, to leap twenty times their own body length, to run up walls, and to walk upside down along ceilings. It was just the nearly getting killed . . .

But being a reptile would be different! Most reptiles were tough and much, much bigger than a creepy-crawly. It would be amazing to become a big scaly predator! That was why they had agreed to help Petty find her missing cubes, so she could crack the REPTOSWITCH code.

"Come on," said Josh. "We're not going to worry about the last cube here. She didn't hide it half a mile from her house."

"We're not going to worry about being watched by government spies, either," grinned Danny. "All that '*Victor Crouch is after me*' business! *That's* all in her head!"

The Wild Things went to scoop creatures out of the pond. Danny mooched along after them. He was bored and trying not to notice Poppy smiling and waving at him with her little glass jar on a bit of pink string. He did *not* want to get to know a dragonfly nymph or a newt—or Poppy. It was a stupid waste of time. He sat down at a picnic bench while the others squelched about by the edge of the water. They oohed and aahed about tiny splodgy brown life-forms.

Danny's stomach rumbled. He noticed a plate left on the table. On it was a sticky chocolate muffin from the wildlife center café. With just

a bit broken off. A rich sweet chocolaty smell was wafting across from it. Danny's mouth watered. He looked around to see if anyone was coming to claim it. Nobody seemed to be. He peered at it a little closer. No wasps on it.

Another chocolaty waft reached him. Danny couldn't resist a moment longer. He grabbed the abandoned muffin and bit into it.

"Mmmmm," he groaned, happily.

"Danny! Come and see this!" said Josh, who was crouching in some bog weed. The other Wild Things had wandered off to the other end of the pond on the other side of some bushes. Danny felt he could bear to show some interest with Poppy no longer goggling at him.

He took the remaining bit of muffin with him and ambled over to his brother.

"See!" said Josh, pointing at a muddy pebble. "A great crested newt!"

"Hey. Wow. I mean, that's, err, great." Danny shrugged.

"What are you eating?" asked Josh, sniffing at his brother.

"Muffin. 'ave some," said Danny, handing the last chunk to his brother.

Josh held up his muddy hands. "Stick it in for me, will you?" he said, opening his mouth. Danny shoved it in.

"Mmm, nice chunky chocolate chips," mumbled Josh.

"Hey!" said a sharp voice behind them. "Who ate my muffin?"

Danny spun around, guiltily. Standing by the picnic bench was . . . oh *no* . . . Petty Potts. Suddenly Danny had bigger things to worry about than being caught for muffin theft.

Petty stared at him and then at Josh, who had turned around too. "Oh dear, oh dear, oh dear," she said, spotting the chocolate crumbs around their mouths.

"Okay, out with it. What *kind* of 'oh dear'?" asked Josh, sounding a little bit squeaky.

"Ummm," said Petty. She looked sheepishly at the little metal container of pellets in her hand and then at the empty plate on the picnic table. "Well . . . "

Then there were two small pops. No further point in explaining. Josh and Danny wouldn't have understood.

When the remaining Wild Things came around from the other side of the pond, they were surprised to see that Josh and his bored brother had disappeared. An old lady was peering anxiously into the pond, saying not very polite words.

Bottom Breathers

"Don't tell me," snapped Josh. "Just don't tell me!" He had his eyes screwed shut and refused to open them.

Danny waggled his feelers in annoyance. "All right. I won't tell you! You can guess!" He climbed up a thick green plant stem. He stared down into the mirror reflection of the water below.

"That was the food that Petty put the S.W.I.T.C.H. pellets into, *wasn't it?*" huffed Josh, still with his eyes shut. "She poked them into a chocolate muffin. Then you went and ate it! And fed it to me too!"

"Sorry," said Danny. "But you should look now. This is pretty cool." His six legs clung to the green blade, and he leaned over for a better look. A rather handsome face peered back up at him from his reflection. His eyes were wide apart and gray, like metal buttons, set into a smooth black face. He had a shiny gray mouth area with some delicate feelers around it. His body was smooth and gently striped with black and dark brown lines. His legs and underparts were a rather nice yellow.

"Check out these legs!" Danny raised up his chunky back pair. They were curved into thick furry segments and felt very powerful. He tried to get a better view of them in the water by leaning off the huge blade of grass a bit further. And then . . .

"Whoaah!"

SPLASH!

He was deep under the water.

And Danny couldn't swim.

The *SPLASH!* made Josh at last open his eyes. He stared in alarm down at the pond below him. He too had arrived in his new creepy-crawly form standing on a wide green leaf, just above the water. The world around him looked totally unlike the normal world. It was absolutely huge, for one thing. An alien spaceship suddenly swooped past

him, making a deafening thrumming noise. Except it *wasn't* a spaceship. It was a dragonfly. It had a stunning blue-green body, sparkling wings, and a nasty killer instinct.

"Danny!" shouted out Josh, ducking under the leaf for safety. There was no reply. Just a widening ring across the water where something had fallen in. Something, Josh realized, that was almost certainly Danny.

"Oh no!" wailed Josh, wondering what to do.

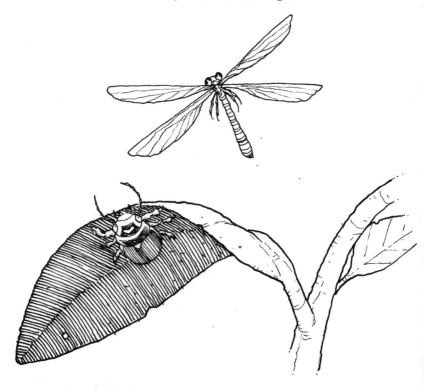

Then he caught sight of his reflection, wobbling below him. He found himself laughing. Actually laughing. For once—just for *once*—he and Danny didn't need to be scared! "It's OK, Danny! I'm coming!" chortled Josh. He dived into the water.

Danny held his breath for as long as he could. He tumbled slowly over and over, sinking down in the green soupy liquid. Fronds of weeds brushed against him. Wriggling see-through creatures scurried away into the gloom. The water was cool and somehow *thicker* than he remembered. It seemed to slide around him in an odd way. He could see in it perfectly well now that he was getting used to it. A forest of underwater trees and shrubs waved gently to and fro. A gigantic brown water snail ambled past him up a stem, blowing a large bubble in his face.

I've got to get to the surface! said a panicky voice in his head. He wished he'd tried harder to learn to swim. He was quite an athletic boy but more of a soccer and baseball kind.

Suddenly there was a booming noise. All the watery trees and bushes waved extra fast as a body tumbled down from the surface. It spun around and began to row quickly toward Danny. Danny stared at it, scared. Meeting other creatures when you were S.W.I.T.C.H.ed was nearly always highly dangerous.

"Danny? Danny!" shouted the other creature. Danny heaved a huge sigh of relief as he recognized Josh shooting toward him. His voice was rather strange and musical through the water.

"Hang on!" said Danny out loud. "How can I breathe a huge sigh of relief? I'm underwater!"

"Yes—but you're a great diving beetle!" laughed Josh.

"Oh, thanks," said Danny.

"No—I mean—that's what we're called,"
explained Josh. "We're great diving beetles. We
can breathe underwater. We carry our own air
pocket with us—see." He jabbed his front leg
against his face. Danny saw a silvery line dimple
in under it. Yes—it was as if they were traveling in
little sacks of oxygen. "We have to go up to the
surface every so often and get more air," explained
Josh. "We sort of suck it up with . . . well . . . with
our butts."

"OK. Whatever you say, you weirdo! But it's
the last time you yell at me for farting!" said
Danny. He turned in the water. He used his
strong back legs like his brother was doing. They
moved like oars on a rowboat. He scudded along
through the water at great speed. Josh sped
along beside him.

"OK—so what's going to eat us?" said Danny,
nervously. Something *always* tried to eat them.

"That's the brilliant bit! Nothing!" Josh was
grinning with his funny insect mouth and
laughing so much there were tiny air bubbles

streaming up from it. "For once, *we* are the predators!"

"You mean to tell me that there's no big ugly fish coming after us?" said Danny.

"Nope. Because this is a small pond. There aren't any big goldfish in it. Just little minnows and sticklebacks and frogs and stuff. *They* won't bother us. And even if they try . . ." He grinned again, which looked rather alarming on a beetle. ". . . we've got a secret weapon!"

"What's that?" asked Danny. "A sting? Nasty bite?" He'd noticed that Josh's jaws looked pretty fierce.

"You'll see," said Josh. He spun around and rowed along again. Danny moved with him. Then he noticed something long and brownish-green scurrying along under a rock.

Danny screamed.

Because Josh was wrong. Josh had got it *badly* wrong.

Lurking under the rock, staring balefully right at Danny was a CROCODILE.

Evil Wet Ones

The crocodile loomed toward him. Its tail rippled
in the water behind it. Its pale yellow belly shone
through the green gloom.

Danny was terrified. "CROCODILE!" he
screamed. Then he let off an absolutely rip-
snorting fart that bubbled through the water like
a mini volcano. "Eww!" Danny had never been
affected by his own farts before. But *this* one was
truly revolting and was spreading in an icky warm
cloud all around him.

Josh doubled back to see what the rather
musical bubbling noise was. "Ah," he said.
"You've found your secret weapon."

"CROCODILE!" gurgled Danny. But the
crocodile was swimming away. Fast.

"Yup," said Josh. "When you think you're being
attacked by a predator, you can let off a really evil

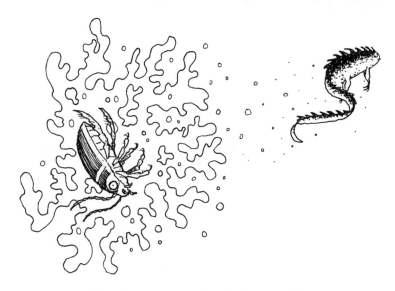

wet one. Another reason the fish don't like you much."

"*I* don't like me much!" gasped Danny. He got his back legs going and powered away from his cloud of stinky wet fart. "But Josh—what about the crocodile? You said we didn't have any predators!"

"You donkey!" laughed Josh. "That was a newt!"

"But . . ."

"You could eat *him* if you really wanted to."

"But . . . why do we need the killer farts if we don't have predators?"

"Well, we haven't got any predators in *here*,"

said Josh. He landed on a large rock and hung onto it with his rather sticky front feet. "But we have up *there*." He looked up through the gloopy skin of the pond's surface. It broke into waves and widening rings every so often and made booming, singing, pinging noises as creatures moved around on it or dived through it. "Herons mostly. They'll try to get us."

"OK—that's one predator too many!" Danny was still shaking after the crocodile scare. "We've got to get somewhere safe!"

"We're probably safer here than anywhere else," said Josh. "We can just wait here until the S.W.I.T.C.H. wears off. Then we'll splash up out of the water when we turn back into boys."

"Haven't you forgotten something?" asked Danny. "Ugh!" He jumped as two small but very ugly wiggly brown things swam past. They stared at him with big dull eyes and grimaced with sharp spiky teeth.

"Watchoo lookin' at?" one of them said and then vanished under some boggy leafy stuff.

"Yeah?" said the other as it followed.

"Dragonfly nymphs," explained Josh. "Don't mind them. They've got issues. They're going to be gorgeous one day, but for now, they've got faces like a smashed toilet."

"Ri-ight," said Danny. "But not predators, eh?"

"Nah—we could take 'em if we wanted. Although they'd put up a fight," said Josh, happily. It was a wonderful experience to be at the top of the food chain for a change.

"Anyway," went on Danny, clinging to the rock alongside Josh. "I said, aren't you forgetting something?"

"What?" said Josh. He eyed a small winged creature struggling on the pond surface. He felt a bit hungry.

"Well . . . let me see . . . Biff, Ollie, and Milo—the pocket freaks. And *lovely* Poppy with her fascinating tub of ants' eggs? What are *they* going to make of you and me suddenly shooting up out of the water? Huh? We'll get banned from Wild Things—definitely!"

Josh ran his front leg across his mouthparts and managed to crease his beetle face into a worried frown. "It is going to be hard to explain," he agreed. "But they've probably nearly finished the pond dipping now. They'll go back inside soon to look at what they've got."

Danny gazed up through the skin of the pond surface. He saw vague shapes and colors moving around. It wasn't unpleasant, sitting here in the pond. OK, the inhabitants weren't too pretty. But at least they weren't trying to snack on him.

"Ooh—ooh! Come and see this!" said Josh. He pushed off the rock and scudded toward some green and brown stems. They snaked up through the water and connected with big, round, flat green and pink platforms on the surface. Lily pads, Danny figured out. Among the stems were some clumps of fine drifting weeds. There was a large silvery bubble lodged in one of these drifts.

"Come on," called Josh, and half of him vanished inside the bubble. Danny hurried after him. Danny noticed another one of those weird nymphs coming at them from under a stick.

PLOLLOP! With great surprise Danny found himself looking into a little dry chamber. It was like a diving bell with a green stick running up through it. Josh was gazing around it, only his head and two front legs poking into the bubble. It wasn't big enough for them to get right into it.

"What is it?" breathed Danny. His voice sounded more normal without all the water pressing in on them.

"It's someone's home," whispered Josh. He noticed some little silky threads wound around the green stick and a small bundle, wrapped tightly in white strands, among them. He wondered whether he should tell Danny what it was. Danny would probably freak out.

"*Whose* home?" asked Danny. But he didn't need to ask. The homeowner was getting back from work. A long, fine brown leg pierced the wall of the air pocket, followed by another. And another.

"Oh . . . I don't like this," gulped Danny. The elegant shape of the legs—four of them now— and the fine hairs running along them looked horribly familiar.

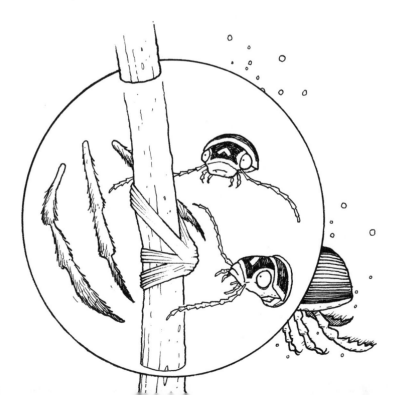

All of a sudden, with a "*thwip*," four more legs, a brown body, and several eyes arrived too. The face around the eyes looked none too pleased to see them there.

"*SPIDER!!!*" shrieked Danny, trying to hide behind Josh. He knew he shouldn't be afraid anymore. After all, he had *been* a spider. He knew they were amazing creatures. It was just hard to forget that he'd once nearly had his insides slurped out like soup from a thermos by one of these creatures while he was a bluebottle trapped in a web.

The spider stared at them, and they stared back.

"It's OK," whispered Josh. "She can't get us. We can eat *her*!"

The spider reared up with her front legs and said, "Well, I call that *rude*!"

"Oh," Josh looked very surprised. His feelers shot up like astonished eyebrows. "Sorry. I didn't think you could understand us. The last spider we met didn't speak English . . ."

"Well—I can!" huffed the spider, her mouthparts flipping about like twitchy fingers. "And if you *think* you can eat me, just try it!"

"Nah . . . not really very hungry, thanks," said Josh. He edged backward out of the air pocket.

Danny continued to stare, appalled, at the spider. She glared back at him angrily. Then he was dragged suddenly out of her home by his rear end. He was delivered back into the water world by his brother. "SPIDERS!" he yelled at Josh. "You didn't tell me there were spiders—down *here*!"

"Sorry," said Josh. "Water spiders. They're cool, though, aren't they? I love that little air pod. Brilliant! This is the best thing we've been!"

Danny shuddered. But scooting powerfully through the water was pretty cool. He began to relax and enjoy himself. "Anything else good about us?" he asked.

"We-ell," said Josh. "There's something you should probably know. It's happened before. We were fine, so don't freak out."

"What?" demanded Danny, his antennae twitching nervously.

"We're girls again."

"NO! No—I refuse to be a girl again!"

"It's no big deal," said Josh, scooting on through the golden-green underwater glade. "When you were an ant girl, you'd never have known if I hadn't told you."

"Apart from all the giggling," grunted Danny.

"Well . . . yeah, there was the giggling," grinned Josh.

"How do you know we're girls?" demanded Danny.

"It's our stripes," explained Josh. "You don't get 'em on boy great diving beetles. Just the girls. Let it go, Danny."

Danny shuddered again. And this time the water shuddered around him. Then it shuddered again. A very BIG shudder.

Josh and Danny spun about and stared at each other. "What's that?" whispered Josh, sounding scared for the first time.

Suddenly there was an ear-splitting crash.
The water churned about wildly, sending
them spinning away from each other. Dancing
fragments of light, waterweed, and tiny see-
through creatures flew in all directions. Danny felt
himself being thrown around uncontrollably.

He shut his eyes, hoping he was returning to
being a boy. And that nobody would see. But
when at last the storm around him calmed down,
he realized he was still a great diving beetle.
Light streamed all around him in a very odd way.
It was coming from above—and around—and
underneath. He tried to swim through it and find
Josh but—CRACK. His head whacked into a solid
force field that sent him spinning back again.
What? Danny tried again. CRACK! And then he
understood why it was so
bright. And why he couldn't
travel for even three pushes
of his legs before being
smacked in the face.

He was in a jar.

He had been pond dipped.

Dippy Chick

Josh lay on his back, waving his legs in the air. For a few seconds he thought he must have morphed back into being a boy. He waited for everyone to start shouting at him for falling in the pond.

But after a few seconds he opened his eyes and realized he was still a beetle. A beetle on its back. On the bank of the pond. A flash of white and gray zoomed across the blue sky. A heron? Josh let off a killer fart and flipped himself over onto his front. He scurried under the shelter of a rocky outcrop. He gasped with shock (and disgust— wow—that fart was *awful*!). Now, he thought, as he surveyed the nearby water and the clumps of bog weed, *where* was Danny?

"Ooooh!" came a familiar voice. "Oooh, Scratch, look! Someone's left chocolate cake! Look! Oh, it's our lucky day!"

Josh peered around the edge of the rock. He
saw two brown rats sniffing at something in
the undergrowth, not far from the picnic bench,
which now rose up like a huge wooden monolith.
"WAIT! STOP!" yelled Josh, scurrying toward the
rats. "DON'T EAT THAT!"

The rats paused and looked over toward him.
"What's *that* about?" murmured one of them.

"Oh, I expect he wants a bit for himself. Well,
tough luck!" said the other one, turning back to
the crumbly brown treat.

"SCRATCH! SNIFF! STOP!" bellowed Josh. All of a sudden he found himself up in the air. His wings had shot out of their cases. He was flying, low to the ground, straight for the rats. He had to save them from being S.W.I.T.C.H.ed. After all, they'd saved him and Danny from death quite a few times!

"Josh? Is that you?" asked Sniff, her delicate spray of whiskers twitching as she peered at the beetle flying toward her. "Oh my! What has she changed you into this time?" Scratch and Sniff knew all about Petty and her S.W.I.T.C.H. spray. They had spent time in her lab, listening in as she talked loudly to herself.

"Yes—yes it is me," said Josh, landing at their feet. "And you *mustn't* eat that cake! Petty's put S.W.I.T.C.H. pellets in it! That's how I ended up like this."

"Oh, you poor love!" clucked Sniff. "She just keeps getting you, doesn't she?"

Josh sighed. "Well, she doesn't *deliberately* try to get us. It just seems to keep happening!"

Sniff gave her husband a *look*. He shrugged back at her. "Whatever you say, dear," she said to Josh. Then she gazed sadly at the cake. Sniff *loved* chocolate cake. Danny or Josh occasionally put some under the shed in their back garden, where Scratch and Sniff lived. Sometimes the rats would come out to eat it with them. When they were in boy form, Danny and Josh couldn't understand what the rats said. But the happy waves of thanks worked well enough.

"Such a shame," sighed Sniff, turning her back firmly on the contaminated cake. "But where's your brother?"

"That's just it," said Josh. He looked around anxiously. "I don't know. He was in the pond with me. Then there was a big sort of waterquake, and now he's gone."

"Well—that's what caused your waterquake," said Scratch. He pointed his brown furry paw at the looming shapes that moved around the pond. "Your human friends were splashing about in the water with jars."

Josh gulped. "Oh. Oh *no*. They were pond dipping! What if Danny's been pond dipped?"

"Well, he might not have been, love," said Sniff. She gave a reassuring smile that revealed her long yellow front teeth. "He might just still be in the water, wondering where you are."

Josh stared at the large green lake. It was going to take a while to search through it. It was probably a better idea to check the pond-dipping jars first. He could fly into the wildlife center building and have a quick look. If Danny wasn't in a jar, he could zip back to the pond and look for him there. Of course, Danny might just turn back into a boy at any time and burst out of the pond anyway. And Josh knew he could change at any time too. He would have to be careful to land as

soon as he felt that peculiar feeling that came just
before the change back occurred.

Then Josh shivered.

"What's up, mate?" asked Scratch.

"If Danny is in a glass jar . . ." murmured Josh,
". . . what's going to happen to him when he
changes back to being a boy?"

The rats and the beetle stared at one another.
They looked as worried as it's possible for two rats
and a beetle to look.

"You'd better get going!" advised Scratch. "We'll
stay here for a while, in case you need us."

"OW!" Danny's head smacked against the lid
of the jar. He had remembered that he had wings.
He had shaken them out of their cases and then
tried to fly up out of the captured pond water. But
he'd only succeeded in knocking himself silly and
splashing back down again.

He noticed something looking at him. It
was one of the ugly little dragonfly nymphs.
"Watchoo tryin' to do?" it sneered at him. "Yous
crazy, huh?"

Danny ignored it and eyed the lid of the jar

through the ever-shifting water. The jar itself had been set down now on an orange shelf. Danny knew it must have been put into the learning center. He could just make out the room beyond his curved glass prison. *How* was he going to get out of here?

"Ain't no good tryin' to get out," said the nymph. "Weez well prizzed up."

"No—I can fly out!" argued Danny.

"Me too, bruv," warbled the nymph. "Just gotta wait a while. Deze wings'll be full growed in a while, yep."

Of course, remembered Danny, Josh had said

these weird little creepy-crawlies turned into dragonflies. This one didn't look as if he was going to change anytime soon though. Danny gulped. *He* could change at any moment, he suddenly realized. Back to a full-sized eight-year-old. But what if he changed now? While he was trapped in a glass jar? What would that do to him? What would give? The glass? Or *him*?

Danny stared out into the wavy lines of the room where he'd hung around, bored, only minutes ago. He thought he had, truly, never been more terrified. There was a musical thud on the other side of the glass as the string attached to the jar flopped down across it. It was pink string.

Danny gulped again. He had seen that pink string before. Where . . . ?

You don't want to know! whispered a voice in his head.

Then a giant, warped, freckly face suddenly wrapped itself around the jar, grinning and steaming up the glass.

No, no, no, whimpered the voice in Danny's head. *I said you didn't want to know!*

But Danny did know. It was too late to block out the awful truth. Poppy had caught him in her pond-dipping jar. Poppy might very well be taking Danny home . . .

Important Points

Petty Potts sat in the sun. Through her binoculars, she watched a pair of rats under the picnic bench. They were definitely sniffing around the S.W.I.T.C.H. pellet-infested cake.

"Come on! Why aren't you eating it?" she whispered. She tapped on the little plastic tub she had brought to collect newly morphed creatures in. She usually had a few seconds to get them while they flapped about in confusion.

Petty huffed to herself. Nothing was going according to plan today. She really hadn't *meant* for Josh and Danny to end up getting S.W.I.T.C.H.ed again. It was all Danny's fault for being such a greedy little so and so. She hoped the brothers were getting along OK as great diving beetles. At least they were a bit less likely to get eaten this time. There wasn't much in a pond that would take on such a ferocious predator.

It was a relief when all the children finished their pond dipping and went back inside. At least when Josh and Danny morphed back into human form again, they wouldn't be in full view of all their friends and the grown-ups who ran the Wild Things group. Petty knew she must sit tight and wait for Josh and Danny to come back. They would need help in explaining what had happened to them. Petty would have to come up with something to convince everyone that they had just fallen into the pond. Maybe while helping her to retrieve her hat or something. Petty took off her hat and threw it out onto the pond, just in case.

She looked at the rats again, while she waited. They were still not eating the cake. Rats, though, were very intelligent. Maybe they'd smelled something and decided not to take the risk. Not that being very intelligent always helped you through life, reflected Petty, with a sigh. *She* was superintelligent. But she had still gotten tricked by her old friend, Victor Crouch, when they worked together in the government's top secret underground labs.

If Victor hadn't stolen her work and burnt out her memory so he could not be caught, she wouldn't be sitting here now, worrying about Josh and Danny. She would have carried on with developing the REPTOSWITCH spray, as well as the BUGSWITCH spray. She would be the most famous scientist in the world.

"Still—*Victor* isn't the most famous scientist in the world either, is he?" muttered Petty to herself, with a smile. "No, Victor! You messed up! What you didn't know was that I always suspected someone would try to steal my work. So I faked all my paper codes and put the *real* codes into my cubes. My wonderful cubes!"

But Petty frowned now. She had all the BUGSWITCH cubes, and she could make her sprays using the code hidden inside them. But the REPTOSWITCH code was not yet complete. She had only five cubes, each with a beautiful hologram of a reptile twinkling in its glass center. Josh and Danny had not yet found the sixth. With parts of her memory burnt out, Petty just could not remember where she'd hidden the cubes. Josh and Danny had managed to find most of them. But without the last one, she would never be able to make any REPTOSWITCH spray.

"Oooooh!" Petty slapped her forehead. "Why did you have to get your memory burnt out, you fool?" she hissed at herself.

A man standing in the bush behind her scratched his chin with a pointed black fingernail. He grinned to himself before moving silently back to the pond dippers in the learning room. Josh flew into the wildlife center learning room, aghast at the amount of noise his wings were making. They were whirring and buzzing, the way beetles' wings often do. He just had to hope that it wasn't very loud to human ears. The last thing he needed was for some fascinated Wild Thing to spot him and try to catch him.

He could see his fellow Wild Things dotted around the room. Huge lumps of colorful human, ambling about and making a lot of noise. Good! The noise would hopefully

disguise the sound his wings were making. The pond dippers had all come back into the learning room now. They had put their jars in a row along an orange shelf, ready to be inspected. Poppy's grandfather was already peering into them. He was holding a notebook and pencil and tapping against the jars with one peculiar pointed black fingernail. Josh flew high over his head. He wished the old man would move away so he could inspect the jars for signs of Danny.

Then Poppy ran up to her grandfather and grabbed his hand. The old man turned away. Josh flew down to the jars and began to work his way along them all. Most of them had lots of weeds, a couple of water snails, and not much else. Most of the pond creatures were way too quick to get caught by pond dippers. The third jar, with the pink string on it, had a bone-crunchingly ugly face peering out of it through a drift of green weeds. A dragonfly nymph. It saw Josh peering in at it. It mouthed "Watchoo lookin' at?" Josh was just about to move on when another face suddenly bloomed through the weed. A great diving beetle.

"Josh! Is that you?!" mouthed the beetle. Josh could just about hear Danny's voice behind the glass.

"Yes! It's me!" he called back. "Danny! You've got to get out of there!"

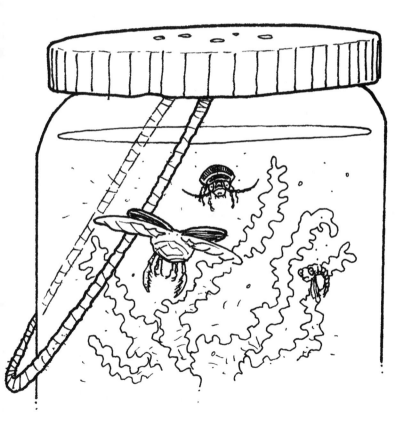

"*Tell* me about it!" yelled Danny. "It's no fun being stuck in here with nymphy boy!"

"Hey! Is youz dissin' me?" demanded Nymphy Boy.

"I can't get out!" yelled Danny. "I've tried to fly up, but the lid's on!"

Josh landed on the lid. It had a couple of air holes punched through the tin. They were too small to get through. And there was no way he could twist off the lid.

"Come on, Josh! Think of something!" begged Danny. "A few more minutes and there's going to be some very nasty jam in this jar!"

"I'll have to get help!" cried Josh, through the air holes. "Scratch and Sniff are out by the pond. And Petty—somehow I'll have to get them to help. Just . . . hold on and don't go anywhere . . ."

"Oh, all right. As you've asked so nicely, I'll just cancel my plans and stay here then!" snapped Danny.

Nymphy Boy loomed up at him, looking even uglier, and spat: "Yo, Beetle Boy. I iz not a boy.

I iz a *girl*."

"Yeah," muttered Danny, with a wince. "Me too, sister."

Jarring Moments

"Scratch! Sniff! I've found Danny!" gasped Josh. He landed under the picnic table in a spray of dust and grass seeds.

"Good!" said Sniff.

"*Not* good!" said Josh. "He's in a jam! Worse . . . he's in a jam *jar*. He's stuck inside it with the lid on. I can't get it off. And he could change back into being a boy at any moment and then . . . and then . . ."

"*Squelch*," shuddered Scratch. Sniff elbowed him in his furry chest. She glared at him.

"How can we get it open?" asked Josh.

"Well," said Scratch. "I don't know if we can open it. But we can certainly knock it off the shelf and smash it. Would that help?"

Josh stared at them. "It's not the *best* way out," he said. "But it's better than nothing." He just hoped that Danny wouldn't get cut in half by shattered glass.

"No time to lose then," said Scratch. He and Sniff ran toward the learning room.

"Be careful!" Josh yelled after them. He knew what they were doing was very dangerous for them. The wildlife center staff could try to trap them if they saw them. Rats might be wildlife too, but the people at the center said there were too many and numbers had to be kept down. Rising up in the air, Josh scouted around for the root of all these disasters—Petty Potts. He saw her sitting on a bench by the pond. Without her usual hat, her silvery hair was blowing around her head.

He buzzed down in front of her face. She didn't flap him away but sat up straight. "Danny? Josh? Is that you?" she said, in a voice that came out loud, deep, and boomy to Josh's beetle ears.

"Follow me!" shouted Josh, although he knew Petty would only hear a buzzing noise. Her giant human ears weren't set up to hear such tiny creatures. If only he could just switch back to human now and explain, life would be much easier. But it was never possible to predict exactly when the change back would happen. And he didn't know how much S.W.I.T.C.H. pellet he had eaten compared to Danny. It could be either one of them first . . .

He turned and flew back to the learning room after Scratch and Sniff. It looked as if the rats were Danny's only chance.

"Where'th Danny gone?" said Poppy to the other Wild Things. "And where'th Josh?"

"I reckon they both went off around the back," said Milo, busy writing notes on his worksheet.

"Well, they thould be back now!" said Poppy, looking annoyed. "I wanted to thow Danny my pond life, Grandad!" she said to the man in the hat. He took his hat off and rubbed around where his eyebrows should have been. Then he put the hat back on again.

"Yes, Poppy," he smiled. "And I really wanted to meet Danny too. And Josh. Don't they live over on Chestnut Lane?"

"Yeth," said Poppy. She led Granddad over to the rows of jars. Then she let out a little shriek. Two furry shapes had just shot up the wall and onto the shelf.

"UGH!" shrieked one of the ladies handing out worksheets. "RATS!"

There were more screams. Then a crash as the rats bashed one of the jars off the shelf and onto the floor, spilling pond water, weeds, and three water snails across the tiles. Then another jar toppled over. This one had pink string on it.

"Oh help! That'th my jar!" squeaked Poppy.

"Oh help!" gurgled Danny as he tumbled through a twisting vortex of water, weed, and madness. The jar was falling. He was a second away from being in a broken glass and pondweed stew. Maybe he'd make it though. Maybe he'd be able to fly away.

WHOMP! SLOOSH!

Suddenly the jam jar stopped falling. A storm of water churned up, down, and around, and then Danny realized the glass was still intact. A hand grasped it firmly, pale long fingers wrapping around. One black, pointy fingernail tapped against the glass.

"Thank you, Granddad!" squeaked Poppy.

Just outside the window, Josh saw the old man in the hat stop Danny's jar from falling. "Oh no!" he moaned, hovering up and down with his wings in a frenzy. "How will we get Danny out now?"

Then he crashed onto the decking below with a loud thud. Everyone in the learning room ran to the window and the door to see what had just fallen. An eight-year-old boy lay on his back, his arms and legs flapping, looking dazed and confused.

"Josh?" said Poppy.

"You all right?" said Milo.

Josh saw Poppy's grandfather lean out behind her, the jam jar still swinging in his hand. He knew it was now or never, while he still had them all surprised and confused. He leaped to his feet. He snatched the jam jar from the old man and ran across the wildflower meadow before anyone could stop him.

Victor-y

For Danny, it was like being in the spin cycle of a washing machine. He no longer knew which way was up. Every so often he would collide with the nymph, who was too dazed herself to say anything. There wasn't time to breathe, let alone menace anyone.

"HEY! COME BACK HERE!" yelled the old man, chasing after Josh. "Come back here with that jar!"

Gosh, thought Josh. He knew it was Poppy's jar, and the old man was her granddad. But he couldn't believe there was a chase going on over a bit of pondweed! Only he knew how special the stuff in the jar was. He needed to get it open now—before Danny changed back. He had to stop running, even if Poppy's granddad caught up.

Josh ducked behind a tree and undid the lid. He tipped the frothy green mess out onto the grass. Danny slid out, landing on his back. His legs were not wiggling. He was quite still.

"DANNY! DANNY!" yelled Josh. He wanted to pick the beetle up and shake it—make it come alive. But he might just squash it in all his panic. "DANNY!" sobbed Josh. "DANNY—PLEASE DON'T BE DEAD!"

"Let me see," said a voice. And Petty Potts knelt down beside him. She put her face close to the soggy beetle. Then she blew on it. The legs waved. But that might just have been in the breeze. Petty looked up at Josh, who was holding his hands over his mouth and blinking with shock. She blew on Danny again. This time a feeler twitched. Then a leg.

Then Danny thumped Petty in the face.

"Ow!" said Petty, holding her nose. "That's the second time you've lumped me on the nose this month!" But she was grinning with relief. Getting whacked in the face as Danny bounced back to boy shape was a price she was willing to pay.

Danny sat up, his clothes soggy and covered with pondweed. He looked at the jar, which lay at an angle with just a little weed left in it. "Oh," he said. "What happened to Nymphy Girl?"

"What?" gasped Josh.

"There was one of those dragonfly nymphs in there with me. Is she all right?" Danny peered into the sludgy weed. He could just make out a tiny, angry face. He chuckled. "We have to put her back," he said.

"Are you telling me that you care about a dragonfly nymph?" said Josh.

"Well—you don't have to make a big thing of it," said Danny, emptying the jar into a nearby watery ditch. "She wasn't my girlfriend. Not really my type. No need to get excited."

"Oh, I don't know," came a strange voice. "I think there's a lot to get excited about."

Everyone stared up into the pale face of the man in the hat. He was smiling down at the scene around the spilled pond water. He scratched the area where his eyebrows should have been with one black, pointed fingernail.

Petty gasped and stood up. "YOU!" she said "YOU! VICTOR CROUCH!"

Josh and Danny gaped at each other. They had never really believed that Victor Crouch existed. They had thought he was all part of Petty's crazy imagination. But here he stood, large as life.

"Hello, Petty," smiled Victor. "You remember me, then."

"Remember you? Why, of course I do, you snake!" she spat. "Victor Crouch—my old friend—the one who tried to steal my work and burn out my memory!"

Victor sighed. "Aaaah, Petty! Still so lovely when you're angry. But you've got it all wrong. Somebody did burn out your memory, that's true. And that's why you can't remember who. It wasn't me. I am your friend."

Petty narrowed her eyes at him.

"Your *friend*," repeated Victor. "And I've come to take you back with me! The government wants you back. We all missed you and your genius brain so much. It's all been a big mistake."

Petty tilted her head to one side, thinking about Victor Crouch's words. She rummaged around in her pockets absentmindedly.

"We're still trying to find out who *did* burn out your memory," said Victor. "And what he did with your work . . . the cubes . . . Petty? The BUGSWITCH cubes and the REPTOSWITCH cubes? Remember? You told me all about them. Where did you find them in the end? Obviously you've got the spray working . . . " He waved his pointy fingernail at Danny and Josh. "Your little friends have been having creepy-crawly adventures with you, haven't they? What brilliant work!"

Petty stared at him. Then she smiled. "Oh, Victor! How could I have been so wrong about you?"

Josh and Danny made faces at each other. Surely Petty wasn't falling for this? Victor Crouch was so creepy he made a slug look good.

"You're not the man I thought you were," sighed Petty. "You're not that at all! You're a COCKROACH! THAT'S WHAT YOU ARE!"

Victor's charming smile vanished. "All right—have it your way, you crazy old witch!" and he pulled a walkie-talkie out of his pocket. "I have agents everywhere! All I have to do is call them. You'll be locked away forever!" He went to press the button on the radio.

There was a short sharp hiss. Petty stood with a spray bottle in her hands. Victor froze as a pale yellow mist of S.W.I.T.C.H. landed on him.

"What? What have you done?" he gasped.

"I told you," said Petty. "You're a cockroach."

Victor vanished. There was a shimmy of a shiny black wing case in the grass. Petty lifted her foot above it.

"Well," she said. "Nice to catch up on old times, Victor. Bye-bye!"

But before her foot could stamp down, Danny leapt forward and pushed her sideways. "PETTY! NO!"

"He's EVIL!" insisted Petty, peering in alarm at the grass. "He'll have us all kidnapped and tortured for the S.W.I.T.C.H. secrets! He cannot be allowed to escape!"

"But that would be murder!" said Danny. "You can't kill people! Not deliberately!"

"Probably wouldn't have worked anyway," said Josh. "Have you ever tried to kill a cockroach? They're armor-plated. They'd survive nuclear fallout. They can live for three months without their *heads*. And you'll never splat them on a soft surface."

Petty dropped to her knees and rummaged in the grass. "He's gone! He's gone already! How could you let him escape? How could you?"

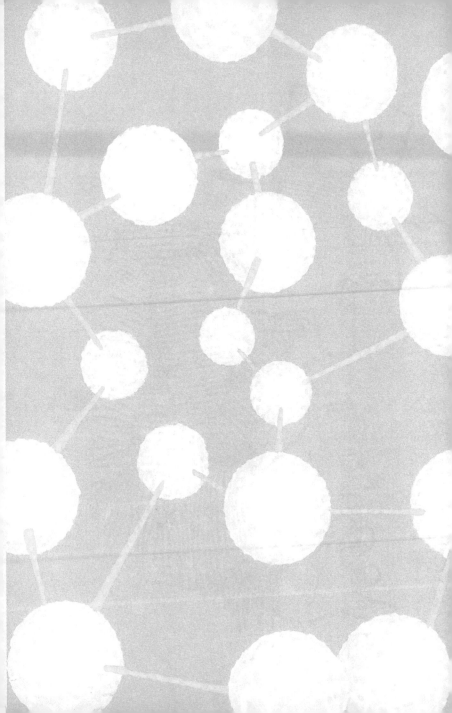

Whose Granddad?

"Well . . . at least he's not going to bother us for a while," said Josh, staring into the grass. "And maybe he'll get eaten anyway . . ."

"I certainly hope so," grumbled Petty, putting the spray bottle back in her pocket. "Good thing I had some spare spray with me. You never know when you might need it." She picked up the walkie-talkie radio that Victor Crouch must have dropped as he turned into a cockroach. "Don't look at me like that! You heard what he said. If he'd pressed the button on this radio and called all his agents, we'd be on our way to a deep, dark prison by now."

"What? Us?" said Danny. "But we're just kids. Nobody would lock us up!"

"Don't you believe it," said Petty. "They would know that you know what I know, don't you know? And if you know, they would want to know what you know and there's no knowing what they'd do to know you know!"

Danny and Josh edged away from her.

"You're crazy," said Danny. "We don't want to play with you anymore! No more helping you out. No more hunting for REPTOSWITCH cubes. You're nuts and you've just tried to kill a man."

"A cockroach," said Petty. "I tried to kill a cockroach. I'm sorry you're upset. Come and see me tomorrow. We'll all have some cake and feel much better."

"I don't like your cake anymore," said Danny.

"Me neither," said Josh.

They turned and ran.

"I always knew this would end in trouble!" puffed Josh as they arrived back at the wildlife center. "And what are we going to say to Poppy? How will we explain what happened to her granddad?"

Poppy was happily doing a drawing of a dragonfly when they got back to the learning room.

"Oh, there you are!" she beamed as they came in.

"What happened to you? Did you fall in the pond and get thoaked?"

"Yes," said Josh.

"Er . . . Poppy," said Danny. "About your granddad . . . um . . . did you see where he went?"

Poppy looked up from her drawing. "My grandad? He'th at home with my gran, thilly!"

"But—but he was just here," said Danny, confused. "He caught your jam jar, remember!"

"Oh, that wasn't my granddad!" said Poppy.

"What?" gasped Josh and Danny, together.

"I never met him until today," she said, going back to her drawing. "He just said he was helping out and that everyone called him Granddad. Why? Is he *your* granddad?"

"No—no, never saw him before . . ." murmured Danny. He and Josh sank down into the chairs next to Poppy, feeling tired and confused.

"Do you like my drawing?" she said to Danny, holding up the paper proudly. It was a good drawing.

"Yeah—it's great," he said.

"I *like* you!" beamed Poppy. "You're thutch fun!

Here—you can have thith!" And she dug her hand in her pocket and pulled out a little plastic bag. "I found thith on your street yethterday. You can have it!"

Danny undid the plastic bag. He stared in wonder at the thing in his hand.

"Thankth . . . I mean, thanks, Poppy," he said. He wandered out of the wildlife center with Josh at his side trying to look into his palm.

Danny gazed around. There was no sign of Petty or—of course—Victor. He opened his hand and showed Josh. It was a cube. A shiny, glass cube, with a hologram of a chameleon twinkling inside it.

The very last cube, containing the last vital part of the code for Petty's REPTOSWITCH spray.

Josh and Danny looked at each other. After all their adventures as creepy-crawlies, after all the times they'd nearly been squashed or eaten, after all the amazing things they'd done, like fly and leap and walk upside down and swim under water . . . NOW, they could move on to being something else even more amazing.

REPTILES.

"But we've just seen Petty try to squash a man dead under her heel," said Josh. "I don't think we should give her this. I don't think we should have anything more to do with her."

"Yes," said Danny. "I think you're right." He shoved the cube deep into his pocket. "Come on, Mom should be waiting for us in the parking lot now."

"Yeah," said Josh, trying to sound normal. "Yeah, we can see her new car! We can have a ride in it and forget everything that's just happened. And pretend it never did happen. That's the best thing!"

They walked around to the parking lot at the front of the Blackthorn Wildlife Center. There was Mom, tooting her horn and waving from her new, shiny green car.

"Look! Look, boys!" she grinned. "Come and get in! I've got a Beetle!"

Top Secret!

For Petty Potts's Eyes Only!!

DIARY ENTRY *621.4

SUBJECT: VICTOR CROUCH IS (POSSIBLY) DEAD!

I cannot believe it! I very nearly KILLED Victor Crouch! I had that nasty little cockroach right under my heel. And then that blasted Danny stopped me! He and Josh seemed to think I was the maniac.

I tried to explain that Victor would have had us all banged up in a government prison for the rest of our lives if he had caught us and told his agents what we knew. But now he's escaped, and if he doesn't get eaten, he will certainly be back.

$$\frac{4 \times \pi^2}{0S-7^*} \searrow \frac{\boxed{P_2}}{0.8} \times \frac{\sqrt{6^2}0/9}{9.\sqrt{50}} = \frac{\cancel{4.198}}{4.197} \atop (548)$$

I do hope Josh and Danny will come over tomorrow so I can explain again. They have to understand the DANGER we're all in!

And of course, I really need their help. We still haven't found the last REPTOSWITCH cube. Without it, I can go no further. I'm sure I will manage to talk them around. After all, they both can't wait to try out being a giant python or an alligator or a monitor lizard.

All boys want that. And even boys who worry about silly things like me stamping on a cockroach. They will want to be a reptile too much to worry for long. Won't they . . . ?

Chin up, Petty. They'll be back.

$$\frac{60}{\text{OVP}}{\pi} \rightarrow \not{R} \rightarrow \frac{1}{2}\underline{s}t^2$$

REMEMBER

Recommended Reading

BOOKS

Want to brush up on your bug knowledge? Here's a list of books dedicated to creepy-crawlies.

Glaser, Linda. *Not a Buzz to Be Found.* Minneapolis: Millbrook Press, 2012.

Heos, Bridget. *What to Expect When You're Expecting Larvae: A Guide for Insect Parents (and Curious Kids).* Minneapolis: Millbrook Press, 2011.

Markle, Sandra. Insect World series. Minneapolis: Lerner Publications, 2008.

WEBSITES

Find out more about nature and wildlife using the websites below.

BioKids

http://www.biokids.umich.edu/critters/
The University of Michigan's Critter Catalog has

a ton of pictures of different kinds of bugs and information on where they live, how they behave, and their predators.

National Geographic Kids
http://video.nationalgeographic.com/video/kids
/animals-pets-kids/bugs-kids
Go to this fun website to watch clips from National Geographic about all sorts of creepy-crawlies.

U.S. Fish & Wildlife Service
http://www.fws.gov/letsgooutside/kids.html
This website has lots of activities for when you're outside playing and looking for wildlife.

CHECK OUT ALL OF THE

#1 Spider Stampede

Eight-year-olds Josh and Danny discover that their neighbor Miss Potts has a secret formula that can change people into bugs. Soon enough, they find themselves with six extra legs. Can the boys survive in the world as spiders long enough to make it home in time for dinner?

#2 Fly Frenzy

Danny and Josh are avoiding their neighbor because she "accidentally" turned them into bugs. But when their mom's garden is ruined the day before a big competition, the twins turn into bluebottle houseflies to discover the culprits. Will they find who's responsible before it's too late?

#3 Grasshopper Glitch

Danny and Josh are having a normal day at school . . . until they turn into grasshoppers in the middle of class! Can they avoid being eaten during their whirlwind search to find the antidote? And will they be able to change back before getting a week of detention?

TITLES!

#4 Ant Attack

Danny and Josh are being forced to play with Tarquin, the most annoying boy in the neighborhood. But things get dangerous when the twins accidentally turn into ants and discover that Tarquin kills bugs for fun.... Can they find a safe place to hide until they turn human again?

#5 Crane Fly Crash

When Petty Potts leaves town, she puts Danny and Josh in charge of some of her S.W.I.T.C.H. spray. Unfortunately, their sister, Jenny, mistakes it for hair spray and ends up as a crane fly. Now it's up to the twins to keep Jenny from being eaten alive.

#6 Beetle Blast

Danny is forced to go with his brother, Josh, to his nature group, but neither of them thought they would turn into the nature they were studying! Both brothers become beetles just in time to learn about pond dipping . . . from the bug's perspective. Can they avoid getting caught by the other kids?

About the Author

Ali Sparkes grew up in the woods of Hampshire, England. Actually, strictly speaking, she grew up in a house in Hampshire. The woods were great but lacked basic facilities like sofas and a well-stocked fridge. Nevertheless, the woods were where she and her friends spent much of their time, and so Ali grew up with a deep and abiding love of wildlife. If you ever see Ali with a large garden spider on her shoulder, she will most likely be screeching, "AAAARRRGHGETITOFFME!"

Ali lives in Southampton with her husband and sons. She would never kill a creepy-crawly of any kind. They are more scared of her than she is of them. (Creepy-crawlies, not her husband and sons.)

About the Illustrator

Ross Collins's more than eighty picture books and books for young readers have appeared in print around the world. He lives in Scotland and, in his spare time, enjoys leaning backward precariously in his chair.